KT-141-948

For John Smith

10th Anniversary Edition printed in 2004 by Ragged Bears
Publishing Ltd, Milborne Wick, Sherborne, Dorset, DT9 4PW

Distributed in the UK by Ragged Bears Ltd, Nightingale House,
England's Lane, Queen Camel, Somerset BA22 7NN
Tel: 01935 851590

Illustrations © 1994 Paul Stickland
Text © 1994 Henrietta Stickland

First published in the United Kingdom in 1994.
Reprinted 1997, 1999 and 2004

A CIP record of this book is available from the British Library

ISBN 1 85714 294 2

Printed in China

# DINOSAUR ROAR!

## PAUL & HENRIETTA STICKLAND

RAGGED BEARS PUBLISHING LIMITED

Dinosaur roar,

dinosaur squeak,

dinosaur fierce,

dinosaur meek,

dinosaur fast,

dinosaur slow,

dinosaur above

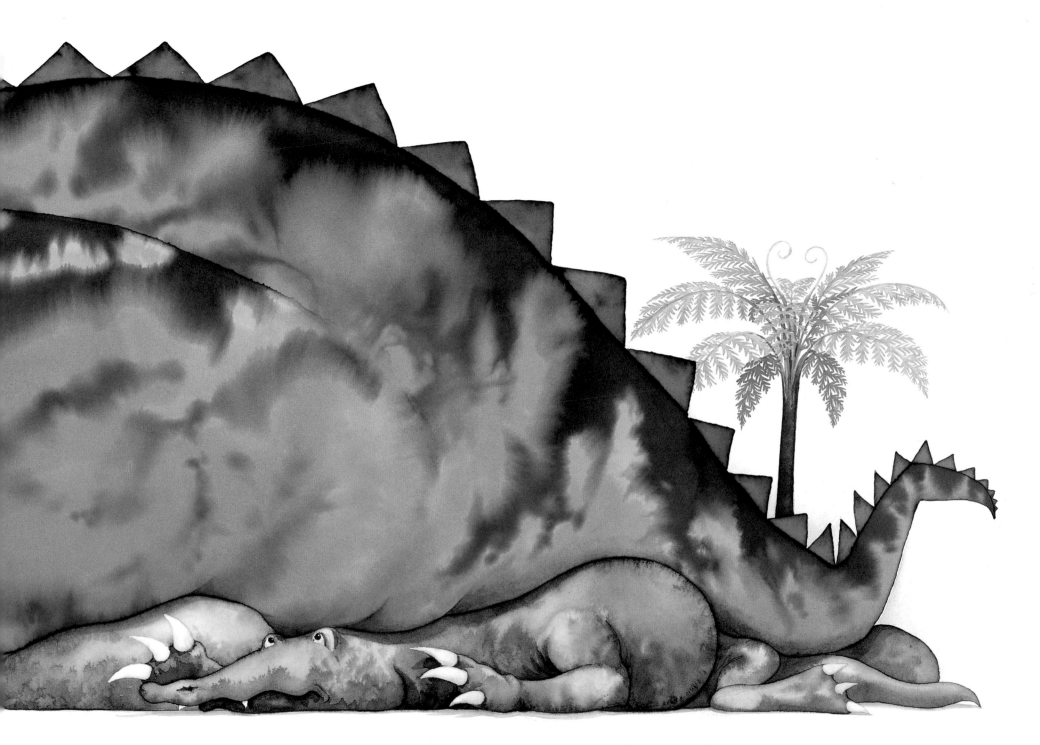

and dinosaur below.

Dinosaur weak,

dinosaur strong,

dinosaur short

or very, very long.

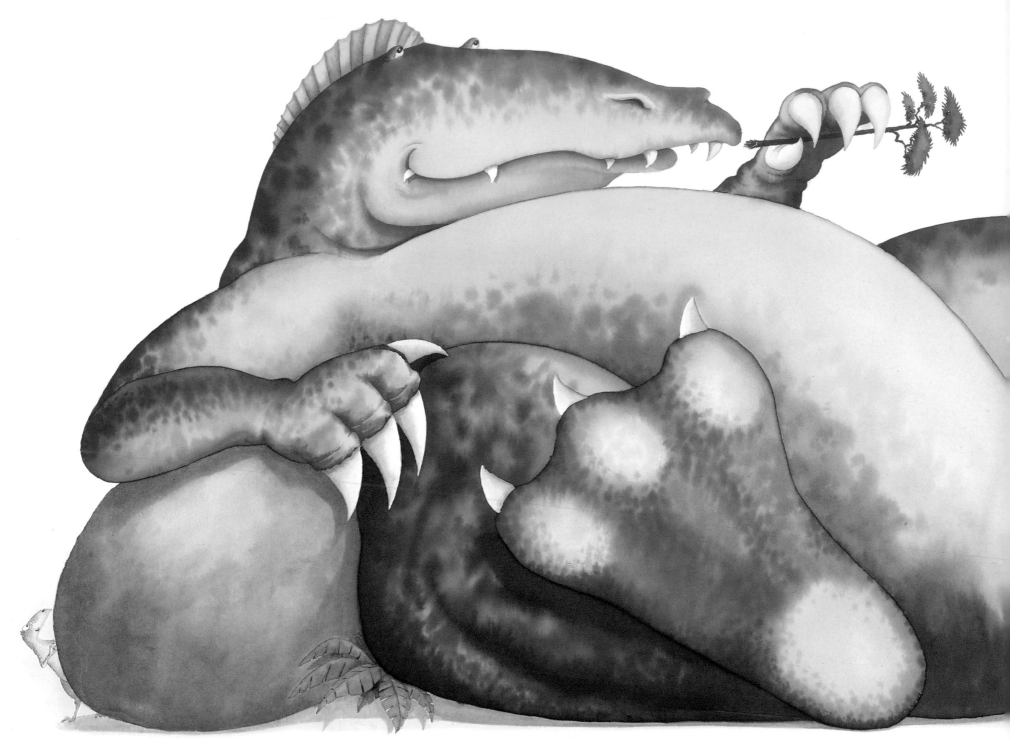

Dinosaur fat,

dinosaur tiny,

dinosaur clean

and dinosaur slimy.

Dinosaur sweet,

dinosaur grumpy,

dinosaur spiky

and dinosaur lumpy.

# All sorts of dinosaurs

eating up their lunch,

gobble, gobble, nibble, nibble,

munch, munch, scrunch!